GARFIELD
AND THE MYSTERIOUS
MUMMY

Created by Jim Davis
Written by Jim Kraft
Designed and Illustrated by Mike Fentz

Published by Troll Communications L.L.C.

Planet Reader is a trademark of Troll Communications L.L.C.

Printed in the United States of America.

10   9   8   7   6   5   4   3   2   1

Garfield's face filled with terror. "Odie! Behind you!" he cried.

Odie spun around. Towering above him was a huge grizzly bear, its fangs bared in a fearsome snarl, its razor claws reaching for the little dog.

Odie's eyes bulged like balloons. Uttering a frightened cry, he collapsed on the floor.

Garfield also fell to the floor . . . but *he* was shaking with laughter.

"Gotcha!" said Garfield. "What's the matter, pal? Haven't you ever seen a teddy bear with teeth?"

Odie looked confused. He looked
at the bear. Then he glared at Garfield
and growled.

Jon Arbuckle watched his pets rolling on the museum floor.

"I wish you boys would stop fooling around," he said. He read the plaque beneath the bear. "'This grizzly bear was bagged by President Theodore Roosevelt while on a hunting trip in Montana. It was presented to the museum in 1903.'"

"Did you hear that, Odie?" said Garfield. "In 1903. That was way before I was born, and before you arrived from the planet Weirdo."

"Let's hurry," said Jon. "The museum closes in an hour. And we have a lot more to see, including that special Egyptian exhibit."

Jon rushed Garfield and Odie from one exhibit to another.

One large gallery was filled with dinosaurs.

"This triceratops skeleton is more than 100 million years old," said Jon.

"Big deal," Garfield replied. "Have you looked in our refrigerator? We have potato salad older than that."

They saw African masks and Eskimo carvings, volcanic rocks and giant bugs, shark teeth and elephant tusks. Finally, they came to a large hall, where the walls were decorated with curious paintings of very flat people.

"This is the Egyptian Gallery," Jon

declared. "There's something here we need to see."

"I hope it's the exit," said Garfield.

Instead of an exit, Garfield saw a statue with the body of a man and the head of a fierce crocodile. He saw ancient

scrolls filled with odd Egyptian picture writing, called hieroglyphics. There was also an interesting collection of Egyptian mummies, some in glass cases, others in mummy-shaped coffins.

At one end of the gallery a large crowd of people had gathered. There, surrounded by a velvet rope, stood a stone pedestal with a glass box on top. Inside the box was a small golden object.

Garfield and Odie peered through the glass.

"You dragged us all this way to see . . . a *nose*?" said Garfield.

"Isn't it awesome, boys?" said Jon. "It's the Nose of Ahmose, one of the most famous Egyptian artifacts in the world."

"Yes," said a voice beside Jon. "It is famous . . . and mysterious . . . and dangerous."

The voice belonged to a small man with a white mustache.

"The Nose of Ahmose," said the little man. "To be more exact, the nose from the funeral mask of the great pharaoh Ahmose, who ruled Egypt from 1570 to 1546 B.C."

"That's about 3,500 years ago," Garfield said to Odie. "You know, back when my ancestors were worshipped and your ancestors were rocks."

"Where's the rest of the mask?" Jon asked the stranger.

The old man shook his head.

"That is the mystery. The mask of Ahmose was stolen from the Egyptian Museum in Cairo in 1953. The thief was clumsy. As he was running away he dropped the mask, breaking off the nose. The police found it lying on the floor."

"Did they ever catch the thief?" Jon asked.

"Sadly, no," the man replied. "The mask of Ahmose has never been found. But at least we have the nose. I finally persuaded the Egyptian Museum to loan it to us for a few months. Soon it will be going back. I do hate to give it up."

"Oh, then you must be —"

The old man extended his bony hand. "Forgive me. I am Dr. Colin Fibbersham, the curator of the museum."

"He's the relic in charge of the relics," Garfield said to Odie.

"Why did you say the Nose of Ahmose was dangerous?" Jon asked.

"According to the legend, the spirit of Ahmose was angered by the theft of his funeral mask. His spirit will not rest until the nose is restored to the mask and the mask is returned to Egypt. They say that at night his mummy stalks the world, searching for his lost property, eliminating anyone who gets in his way. Who knows? Perhaps the spirit of Ahmose is lurking in this

very gallery, plotting his revenge."

Garfield, Odie, and Jon looked nervously at all the mummies, then at the nose.

"That's a spooky story," said Jon.

"I'm sorry if I frightened you," Dr. Fibbersham replied. "The Nose of Ahmose casts a very powerful spell, especially on an old collector like me. But it's nearly closing time, so I must go. Enjoy the rest of your visit."

Dr. Fibbersham turned and walked away.

"We still have a few minutes left," Jon said. "Let's look at more of this Egyptian stuff."

"If you want to look at old stuff, let's go look at your grandma!" snapped Garfield. "At least she gives me cookies. These mummies just give me the creeps!"

Garfield was tired. And he was bored. He saw Odie standing beside a mummy case. A wicked grin spread across Garfield's face. Quickly, he slipped around the other side of the case. Bending down so Odie couldn't see him, Garfield began shaking the case. In a spooky voice he chanted, "Ahmose wants his nose! Ahmose wants his nose!"

Odie turned, took one look at the rocking mummy, and raced out of the Egyptian Gallery.

"Odie! What's the matter with you?" cried Jon. "Come back!" He ran after the frightened pup.

Garfield sighed with satisfaction. "I knew the mummy would scare the dummy," he said. "Now, how do I get out of here?"

Odie didn't know where he was heading, and he didn't care. The panicked pup skittered across the marble floors. Swerving wildly around other visitors, he barely avoided crashing into priceless artifacts.

A man in a uniform blocked his path. "Whoa, doggy! Whoa!" the security guard ordered as he dropped to his knees.

But Odie's fear was stronger than any order. The pooch leaped into the air, stepped on the guard's cap, vaulted over him, and kept on running. Before the guard could rise, Jon Arbuckle raced up, stepped on the man's hat, and leaped over him, too!

"Hey! Stop!" cried the guard.

"Sorry," Jon called over his shoulder. "I've got to catch that dog!"

The security guard ran after Jon and Odie. Diving, he tackled Jon.

"I'm afraid you're going to have to leave, sir," said the guard, lifting Jon up by his shirt collar and walking him toward the exit.

"What about my pets?" asked Jon.

"When the museum closes, I'm sure they'll find their way out," said the guard.

"You don't know Odie," said Jon. "He has trouble finding his way out of a closet."

While Jon was being escorted to the door, Odie was finally slowing down. He looked around and was relieved to find no mummies nearby. But he had no idea where he was.

Odie kept walking, hoping he would spot someone or something familiar. But everything in this part of the museum seemed strange to him. Finally, he saw some animals lined up behind a velvet rope. Trotting over, Odie barked a friendly greeting.

The animals just stared at him.

Odie cocked his head to one side, then the other. Finally, he shrugged. At least they weren't trying to chase him. Odie ducked under the rope and jumped up beside a bird with a hooked bill and stubby wings.

A short time later, two boys came into the room. They stood on the other side of the rope, examining Odie and the other animals.

"These animals are extinct," said one of the boys. He began reading the plaques in the exhibit.

"Here's a dodo bird," said the other boy, pointing to the bird beside Odie.

"It sure is funny looking," said his friend. "No wonder they called it a 'dodo.'"

DODO
BIRD

TASMANIAN
TIGER

Then both boys looked at Odie.

"What's this guy supposed to be? There's no sign."

They stared at the pup, who stared back without blinking.

"He certainly looks goofy," said one.

"I've got it!" the other declared. "He's a 'dodo dog.'"

"Dodo dog! Dodo dog!" the boys repeated, laughing, as they walked away.

After the boys left, the museum grew quiet. Odie wished Garfield and Jon would find him. He wished those two boys would come back. Finally, he heard footsteps.

But it was only a man with his coat collar turned up around his face. He walked quickly to a nearby alcove and opened a door. The door led to a closet. The man stepped inside.

Odie hoped the man would come out. If he came out, Odie would bark at him. Maybe the man would talk to him.

But the closet door stayed shut. The man never came out.

Now it was getting dark inside the museum. Odie scrunched down beside the dodo, resting his chin on his paws. He kept his eyes wide open. There might be mummies about.

Garfield's search for the exit led him to an unfamiliar corridor filled with a familiar smell.

"Pizza!" shouted Garfield.

At the end of the corridor was a door marked "Museum Security." The door was open slightly. Garfield slipped inside.

The pizza box rested on a desk. "The long-lost Pizza of Giza has been found!" Garfield announced. He strolled over to the desk, flipped open the box, and was about to help himself to a big slice—when there was a sudden and

painful yank on his tail.

"The dog made me do it!" cried Garfield, throwing up his paws. Slowly, he turned his head.

A scowling female cat had her paw wrapped firmly around his tail. "Who gave you permission to be in this area?" she demanded.

"Uh, nobody, actually," muttered Garfield. "You see—"

"This area is strictly for museum personnel only."

"Yes," Garfield agreed, "but I smelled the pizza—"

"Name?" the other cat asked.

"Pepperoni with extra cheese," Garfield answered.

She made a face. "Not the pizza's name. *Your* name."

"Oh. It's Garfield."

The lady cat let go of Garfield's tail. "Here's the way I see it, Garfield. You've been caught in a restricted area while committing a 2-11. That's the 'unlawful use of a slice of pizza.' The penalty for this is . . . is . . . Oh, I knew I couldn't do this with a straight face." She giggled.

Garfield relaxed.

"I've always wanted to make an arrest like that," the lady cat continued. "You know, like they do on TV? But I never get the chance around here."

"Are you a police cat?" asked Garfield.

"Sort of. My regular partner, Joe, thinks of me as his pet. But I like to think of myself as a 'security assistant.' Joe's on vacation now, so I'm working with Pete, his temporary replacement. Well, I'm not really working with him. Pete's pretty much of a loner. He probably doesn't even like cats. Twice already he's forgotten my nightly saucer of milk. Plus, Pete snoops around a lot. I saw him coming out of the curator's office the other night. We're not supposed to enter the offices, except in cases of emergency. Joe never goes in the offices. There's something strange about Pete, I can feel it. Know what I'm saying?"

"Not really," said Garfield. "Do you mind if I eat while you babble?"

"Help yourself," said the cat. "Of course, it's not my pizza. I don't know how Pete might feel about it. My name's Cleo, by the way. Short for Cleopatra. Sort of fits, with the museum and all, don't you think?"

Garfield nodded and took another bite.

"Sorry I had to rough you up, pal,"

said Cleo. "But I can't be too careful. This special Egyptian exhibit is a security nightmare. There are weird things going on around the museum these days. Strange noises at night. One of our mummy coffins is missing. Mummies on the prowl. I have to stay alert."

Garfield gulped. "You mean that story about the spirit of Ahmose is true?"

"Maybe. Maybe not. So far it's just a rumor. But we have to be ready for anything."

Garfield quickly grabbed another slice of pizza. "Well, thanks for the snack," he said. "I'll be going now."

"Going where?"

"Home, of course," Garfield said.

"Negative, Garfield," Cleo replied. "You're not going anywhere."

Garfield heard slow, heavy footsteps coming down the corridor.

"Who's that?" he said anxiously. "Is it the mummy? He can have the nose. He can take any body parts he wants, as long as they're not mine!"

The door opened. Garfield dove behind Cleo.

A middle-aged man in a security officer's uniform entered the room. He sat down at the desk and began writing in a notebook. With his free hand he picked up the last slice of pizza.

"Well, Cleo," he said, without

looking up, "the museum doors are locked. Not a very busy evening. Just some nut chasing his dog through the museum. Had to throw him out. He begged me to keep an eye out for his dog and cat. I've got all the information written down here."

"Good work, Pete," said Cleo.

Pete felt for another slice of pizza, but came up empty-handed. He looked

at the box, then at Cleo. "Cleo, what happened to my pizza?"

Cleo stepped aside and pointed to Garfield. "The culprit is already in custody," she said.

"Go easy on me, please," Garfield begged. "I haven't done anything like this since yesterday."

Pete grunted in surprise. "This must be the cat that Arbuckle guy was talking about. We'll have to give him a call. I wonder what happened to the dog? Probably found his way home by now, I guess. Dogs are good at that."

"You don't know Odie," Garfield said. "He needs a map to find his way out of bed."

Pete stood up. "Guess I'd better check on a few things."

"I'll go with you," said Cleo.

"Stay here, Cleo," said Pete,

blocking the doorway. "We can't have you roaming the halls at night."

"But Joe always lets—" Before she could finish, Pete had closed the door behind him.

"See what I mean?" Cleo said to Garfield. "There's something fishy about that guy. I heard him talking on the phone last night. And he was speaking French! Why would a security guard be speaking French?"

"Maybe he called France to order some fries," Garfield suggested.

"I couldn't understand what he was saying, but I recognized the name 'Ahmose.' That name came up a lot."

"That's the pharaoh's name," said Garfield.

"Exactly," said Cleo. "I think we'd better check on what Pete's checking on."

The museum, which earlier had been bright and interesting, was now dark and forbidding. The strange statues and massive skeletons loomed like monsters in the shadows.

Garfield's fear kicked inside him like a kangaroo in a closet. "I think we should go back to the office," he whispered to Cleo. "I just remembered something."

"What?" she asked.

"I'm a coward."

"Don't worry about it," purred Cleo. "You're with me."

The two cats padded softly through the maze of rooms that made up the museum. Corridors and galleries seemed to shoot off in all directions, yet somehow managed to reconnect. After eight years on the job, Cleo knew the museum's layout like Garfield knew the way to the fridge.

"I can't believe we haven't run into Pete," said Cleo, frowning. "If he were following Joe's routine, we'd have seen him by now. I don't like it."

"Maybe Pete and the mummy went out for more pizza," Garfield suggested.

They walked a little farther, not saying anything.

"Well," said Garfield, breaking the silence, "there doesn't seem to be anything unusual going on."

At that moment, there was a tremendous crash!

"Except for that."

"It came from the Arms and Armor exhibit," said Cleo. "Let's roll!"

"Let's not," Garfield pleaded. But, not wanting to be left alone, he had to follow her.

The armor room was close by.

When they peeked into the room, Garfield and Cleo saw silver and gold arms and legs scattered all over the floor.

"Wow," said Garfield. "It looks like King Arthur's court exploded. What could have caused this?"

"Look for evidence," Cleo ordered.

They had barely begun searching when they heard a strange noise. Looking around, they saw half a suit of shiny armor—helmet, breastplate, and arms—rattling on the floor. Suddenly,

the armor stood up. The half-knight seemed to look around. Then it began to wobble toward Garfield and Cleo!

"Uh, shouldn't we be leaving now?" Garfield asked.

"No can do," snapped Cleo. "It's my job to catch this bucket of bolts. Try not to get in the way."

"If you need me, I'll be fainting in the corner," said Garfield.

Cleo pointed at the advancing armor. "Freeze, buster, or I'll turn you into scrap metal!"

The half-knight halted. Then it began to whimper.

"Wait a minute," said Garfield. "I recognize that whine." He moved to the mysterious armor and carefully lifted the visor of the helmet.

"Cleo, may I present Sir Droolalot. Also known as my old pal, Odie."

Odie barked a happy greeting.

"Same to ya, Odie," Cleo replied. "I'm afraid you made a mess of this exhibit. Dr. Fibbersham won't like it."

Garfield helped Odie out of the armor. "What were you doing inside this tin can anyway?"

Odie put his paws over his eyes.

"Hiding?" guessed Garfield.

Odie nodded.

"Hiding from what?" Cleo asked.

Odie wrapped his tongue around his face.

"A mummy?" Cleo asked.

"Arf!" said Odie.

"Odie, that mummy wasn't alive," said Garfield. "I was just playing a joke on you."

Odie nodded vigorously.

"No, Odie," Garfield countered. "The whole thing is just a legend."

Odie began barking excitedly. He pointed to the doorway.

Garfield and Cleo turned, and a bolt of horror flashed through both of them. The legend had come to life!

The mummy marched toward the three terrified animals. His foot struck a medieval helmet. The mummy halted. He looked at the armor scattered on the floor. "Mmmmm!" the mummy grumbled angrily.

"Sounds like someone got up on the wrong side of the coffin," said Garfield. "I think we'd better go."

"A good cop doesn't run from danger," said Cleo.

The mummy grabbed a sword from the wall and swung it at the pets.

"But a smart cat knows when to

scram!" shouted Cleo. "Let's get out of here!"

Garfield, Odie, and Cleo bolted from the room, with the mummy shuffling after them. They ran without looking back. The effort was especially hard on Garfield. "I almost died of fright," he gasped. "Now I'll probably die of sweat!"

"Turn here!" Cleo ordered as they

raced toward another hallway. "I know a shortcut through the music room."

The three pets swung left down the hallway. Cleo slowed to a trot, then stopped. She listened. No footsteps sounded in the hallway behind them. "I think we lost him," Cleo whispered.

"He . . . He . . . moves pretty fast for a dead guy," said Garfield, trying to catch his breath. "Of course, he's been resting for 3,500 years."

"We've got to keep moving," said Cleo. "That mummy could be anywhere around here. And we've still got to find Pete."

They trotted through the History of Music exhibit and the shrunken head display, staying alert for any sign of the mummified monster. Turning out of another gallery, the terrified trio entered one of the main corridors of the museum.

"Egyptian Gallery, dead ahead," Cleo declared.

Garfield was just about to comment, when a figure stepped from the shadows twenty feet in front of them.

"Undead, dead ahead!" Garfield screamed.

Garfield tried to put on the brakes, but the museum's marble floors were slick, and his legs flew out from under him. The fat cat barreled into Odie, who upended Cleo. Then the pile of pets slid right into the mummy, bowling him over.

A dazed Garfield found himself lying face-to-face with his foe.

Garfield smiled in terror. "How's it going, Your Mummyness?" he asked. "Build any good pyramids lately?"

"Urrrrrr!" growled the mummy, snatching hold of the fat cat.

At that instant Odie and Cleo leaped on the mummy, forcing him to drop their friend. Garfield sprang to his feet, grabbed Odie by the paw, and started running. Then they heard a cry.

"Let go of me, you bag of bones! You're under arrest!"

It was Cleo. The mummy had her by the ankle!

"Cleo!" cried Garfield.

"Garfield! Partner!" Cleo shouted as the mummy carried her off.

Garfield and Odie watched in horror as the mummy disappeared.

"Urf?" said Odie, looking both sad and scared.

Garfield put his arm around his pal. "Don't worry, Odie," said Garfield with determination. "We're not going to abandon Cleo. I'll find a way to rescue her. And when I do, that mummy will be calling for his mommy!"

Slowly and fearfully, Garfield and Odie crept after Cleo and the mummy. The two pets peeked around every corner and shivered at every shadow. In the Egyptian Gallery they scampered from statue to statue. But passing through the mummy collection was the most nerve-racking experience of all!

"I hope old Fossil Face doesn't have any buddies around here," Garfield whispered, his eyes darting from one mummy to another.

They had worked their way to the

opposite end of the gallery when Garfield saw something that made him gasp.

"Odie! Look!" Garfield pointed to the pedestal where the Nose of Ahmose was displayed. The top of the glass case had been removed. The pharaoh's golden nose was gone!

"Looks like the freaky pharaoh got what he came for," Garfield said to Odie. "Now maybe he'll go looking for the rest of the mask and leave this museum alone. But we've still got to find Cleo before something bad happens to her. Odie, that nose of yours must be good for something besides sneezing. I want you to sniff out that mummy. Can you do it, pal? Can you prove that you're more than a flea colony with feet? Can you use *your* nose to find Ahmose?"

"Ruff!" said Odie, giving Garfield a thumb's up.

"Then do it, dog!"

Odie laid his nose on the marble floor and began sniffing. He stood up. His face started to wriggle.

"AHCHOO!"

Garfield shook with impatience. "Be a bloodhound, not a dudhound!" he begged. "Please, try again!"

Odie gritted his teeth and put his nose to the floor. He sniffed. He sniffed again. His tail started twitching. Soon he was sniffing and snuffling across the museum floor.

"That's a boy, Odie!" Garfield cheered. "Find that pharaoh!"

The search wasn't easy. Odie was still Odie, after all. First he tracked down a stuffed monkey in the rain forest exhibit. Then he sniffed out an old shoe in the museum's Lost and Found.

Finally, Odie sniffed his way to a door marked "Janitor." He stared at the door. There was something vaguely familiar about it.

Garfield stared at the door, too.

"What's this?" he asked. "Another

wild goof chase? Odie, we're looking for a
mummy, not a mop! Try again!"

But Odie began barking and
pointing at the door.

"You think there's something in
there?"

Odie nodded his head urgently.

"Okay," said Garfield. "I'll open it, if you insist."

Garfield turned the doorknob and pushed the door open. It was dark inside. Garfield flicked on the light.

"See?" said Garfield. "There's nothing here but mops and brooms and cleaning stuff. Let's go. We're wasting time."

But Odie bounded into the closet and started rooting around in the back.

"Odie, get your nose out of that closet and get back on the trail!" Garfield yelled.

Just then, Odie's nose touched a switch hidden behind some old boxes. With a click, the rear wall of the closet swung open.

Garfield scrambled over boxes until he stood beside Odie. "A secret passage," he said, peering into the dark tunnel beyond the door. "Do you think we should check it out?"

Odie nodded.

"You know this may be dangerous."

Odie nodded again.

"You're not afraid, are you?" Garfield asked.

Odie shook his head.

"Good," said Garfield. "Then you go first."

Garfield and Odie moved slowly, feeling their way along the passage. They inched forward until they could see a dim light glowing in the tunnel. The light grew brighter. Finally the two pets reached an open doorway at the end of the tunnel.

They found a large room filled with paintings, statues, and all sorts of treasures. "It's like a mini-museum," Garfield whispered.

Garfield and Odie threaded their way through the stacks of treasure. Suddenly, Garfield put a paw on Odie's arm.

In the center of the room was a mummy coffin. Close by they saw Pete, sitting on a chair. He was tied up, with tape across his mouth. Cleo was on the floor beside Pete. She was tied up, too. And standing behind a nearby table was . . . the mummy!

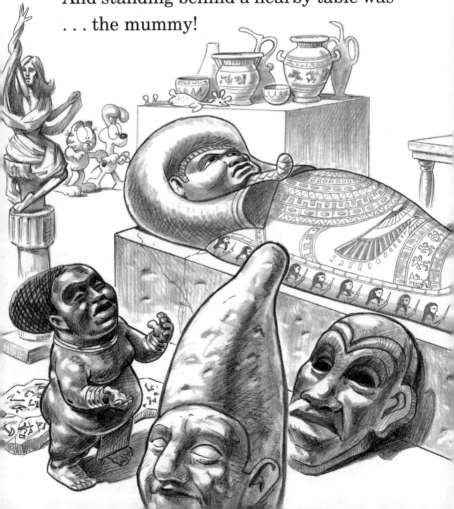

Cleo turned to Pete. "Don't worry, Pete," she said. "We'll get out of this. Garfield will get some help. He seemed fairly bright, though a bit out of shape."

Garfield made a face. "That's not true," he said to Odie. "I'm *really* bright and *completely* out of shape!"

The mummy finished his business at the table. Turning his back on his captives, he reached behind his head. With a sharp tug, he pulled one end of his wrappings free. Then he began to unwind the cloth.

Garfield grimaced. "I can't watch," he whispered. "After 3,500 years this guy's face is going to look like worm stew!"

The mummy continued to unwind the cloth. Slowly the top of his head appeared. Then his eyes and nose. Finally, his chin.

The mummy turned to face Pete and Cleo.

"Well, I'll be a mummy's uncle," said Garfield.

"Dr. Fibbersham!" Cleo gasped.

Dr. Fibbersham picked up a silver candlestick. "I'm so sorry I had to strike you with this," he said to Pete. "But I'm afraid I had no choice. Your snooping led you to my little treasure room. It's taken me a lifetime to collect all of these beautiful things, and I'm not about to give them up. Especially not now."

The doctor moved to the table. On it was a small package wrapped in cloth. Beside the package was a large wooden chest. Dr. Fibbersham picked up the smaller object and undid the cloth.

"The Nose of Ahmose," said the doctor, holding it up to admire. "At last my mistake will be made right."

Dr. Fibbersham placed the nose

gently on the cloth. Then he opened the wooden chest. Inside was the golden face of a pharaoh who had died thirty-five centuries before. With great care Dr. Fibbersham placed the golden nose back on the face.

"The mask of Ahmose!" he declared excitedly. "Just as it looked when the great pharaoh died in 1546 B.C. Just as it looked when I first saw it in the Egyptian Museum in Cairo."

Dr. Fibbersham turned to Pete and Cleo. "Isn't it beautiful?" he said. "I hope you'll take a good look. Because I'm afraid it will be one of the last things you'll ever see."

The doctor crossed to the mummy coffin. Straining, he lifted the heavy lid.

"In a few minutes, Pete, I'm going to place you in this coffin," he explained. "And there you will stay. You should feel honored. Though you are a lowly security guard, you will be entombed in a coffin made for a king."

Pete glared at his captor.

"And just as with the ancient pharaohs, your cat will be buried with you."

"You'll never get away with this," said Cleo, but she didn't sound completely certain.

"Tomorrow the Nose of Ahmose will be missing from the museum," Dr. Fibbersham continued. "But so will you. I'm afraid the police will think *you* stole it, Pete. I will have to agree with them. And now, if you will give me a few minutes to get out of the rest of my mummy wrappings, we can get on with the more serious business of getting you out of the way forever."

"Odie, these guys are in big trouble," said Garfield. "We've got to do something, and fast!"

Garfield watched Dr. Fibbersham unwinding his mummy cloth. "I have an idea!" said Garfield. "Come on!"

Slowly Dr. Fibbersham dragged Pete over to the mummy coffin. "Whew," gasped the doctor, wiping his forehead. "I'm not so young anymore. I hope I still have the strength to tip you into the coffin."

The doctor took several deep breaths and stretched his back. Then he bent down and grasped Pete beneath the arms.

Just then, a strange moaning growl echoed from the tunnel.

Dr. Fibbersham stood up. "What could that be?" he asked.

"Whatever it is, I hope it eats you," snarled Cleo.

They heard it again, louder this time. "GRRRRROOOOOOOOO!"

"Dear me," said the doctor. "I can't imagine . . ."

At that instant, a mummy lurched into the room.

"GRRRRR!" the mummy growled.

"But . . . this can't be!" Dr. Fibbersham declared. "The spirit of Ahmose . . . It's nonsense! It's just a legend!"

"Well, that legend seems pretty mad at you," said Cleo.

The mummy stomped toward the curator.

"No! No!" said Dr. Fibbersham, backing away. "I didn't mean to steal your mask! You can take it back!"

But the mummy continued to advance relentlessly with its arms outstretched.

"No! Go away!" cried the curator. "Help!"

Step by step, the mummy drew closer. The curator leaned back in horror. He fell into the open coffin. Quickly, the mummy slammed the heavy lid shut.

Pete and Cleo, who had been amazed by the sight of a second living mummy, were even more astonished when the new mummy seemed to split into a top half and a bottom half. Then both halves unwrapped themselves to reveal . . .

"Garfield and Odie!" cried Cleo. "You saved us!"

"It was nothing, ma'am," drawled Garfield. "We're just two pets who like to dress up like mummies and catch dangerous criminals." He looked at his mummy wrappings littering the floor. "And by the way, tell the janitor we're sorry for using up all the toilet paper."

Garfield and Odie untied Pete and Cleo. Then Pete hauled Dr. Fibbersham out of the coffin, handcuffed him, and marched him back to the security office. First Pete called the police; then he phoned Jon Arbuckle.

Jon rushed down to the museum. He was relieved to see his pets again. He gave Garfield and Odie a big hug.

"Hey!" said Garfield, squirming in Jon's embrace. "Crimefighters don't go for all this mushy stuff!"

Pete held out his hand. "I'm Inspector Peter LeGrand," he said.

"We've met," Jon replied. "You're

74

the security guard who threw me out of the museum, remember?"

"I do. But I'm not a security guard. I'm a special agent with Interpol, the international police force based in Paris, France. My specialty is recovering stolen art treasures."

"No wonder he was snooping around," said Cleo.

"We had suspected Dr. Fibbersham for a long time," Inspector LeGrand explained. "But we had no proof. Thanks to your pets, I was able to bag a thief and recover the mask of Ahmose and a great many other stolen treasures. The museums of the world will be forever grateful to Garfield and Odie."

"That's okay," said Garfield. "It's only what we deserve."

"The Egyptian government will be especially eager to express their thanks," Inspector LeGrand added.

"Really?" said Garfield. "I wonder what they have in mind? You know, my face would look very attractive on that Great Sphinx of theirs."

"I want to thank you, too, Garfield," said Cleo, offering her paw.

"For a rookie, you sure came through in the clutch. You can be my partner anytime."

"Thanks," Garfield replied. "But I already have a partner." He winked at Odie. "He may not be a pharaoh. But he's got a pretty fabulous nose!"